AF575897

A Robbie Reader

HAILEE STEINFELD

Joanne Mattern

Mitchell Lane
PUBLISHERS
2001 SW 31st Avenue
Hallandale, FL 33009
www.mitchelllane.com

Printing 1 2 3 4 5 6 7 8 9

A Robbie Reader Biography

Aaron Rodgers
Abigail Breslin
Adam Levine
Adrian Peterson
Albert Einstein
Albert Pujols
Aly and AJ
Andrew Luck
AnnaSophia Robb
Ariana Grande
Ashley Tisdale
Brenda Song
Brittany Murphy
Bruno Mars
Buster Posey
Carmelo Anthony
Charles Schulz
Chris Johnson
Clayton Kershaw
Cliff Lee
Colin Kaepernick
Dak Prescott
Dale Earnhardt Jr.
Darius Rucker
David Archuleta
Debby Ryan
Demi Lovato
Derrick Rose
Donovan McNabb
Drake Bell & Josh Peck
Dr. Seuss
Dustin Pedroia
Dwayne Johnson
Dwyane Wade
Dylan & Cole Sprouse
Ed Sheeran
Emily Osment
Ezekiel Elliott
Hailee Steinfeld
Hilary Duff
Jamie Lynn Spears
Jennette McCurdy
Jeremy Lin
Jesse McCartney
Jimmie Johnson
Joe Flacco
Johnny Gruelle
Jonas Brothers
Keke Palmer
Larry Fitzgerald
LeBron James
Mia Hamm
Michael Strahan
Miguel Cabrera
Miley Cyrus
Miranda Cosgrove
Philo Farnsworth
Raven-Symoné
Rixton
Robert Griffin III
Roy Halladay
Shaquille O'Neal
Story of Harley-Davidson
Sue Bird
Syd Hoff
Tiki Barber
Tim Howard
Tim Lincecum
Tom Brady
Tony Hawk
Troy Polamalu
Tyler Perry
Victor Cruz
Victoria Justice

Library of Congress Cataloging-in-Publication Data
Names: Mattern, Joanne, 1963– author.
Title: Hailee Steinfeld / by Joanne Mattern.
Description: Hallandale, FL : Mitchell Lane Publishers, 2018. | Includes bibliographical references and index.
Identifiers: LCCN 2017024488 | ISBN 9781680201314 (library bound)
Subjects: LCSH: Steinfeld, Hailee. | Actors—United States—Biography. | Singers—United States—Biography.
Classification: LCC PN2287.S6775 M38 2017 | DDC 791.4302/8092 [B] —dc23
LC record available at https://lccn.loc.gov/2017024488

eBook ISBN: 978-1-68020-132-1

ABOUT THE AUTHOR: Joanne Mattern is the author of many books for children on a variety of subjects, including history and biography. She has written many biographies for Mitchell Lane. Joanne loves to learn about people, places, and events and bring historical figures to life for today's readers. She lives in New York State with her husband, children, and several pets.

PUBLISHER'S NOTE: The following story has been thoroughly researched and to the best of our knowledge represents a true story. While every possible effort has been made to ensure accuracy, the publisher will not assume liability for damages caused by inaccuracies in the data, and makes no warranty on the accuracy of the information contained herein. This story has not been authorized or endorsed by Hailee Steinfeld.

TABLE OF CONTENTS

Chapter One
A Difficult Role 5

Chapter Two
A Young Actress 9

Chapter Three
True Grit 13

Chapter Four
New Horizons 17

Chapter Five
Hailee's Real Life 23

Chronology 27
Filmography 28
Find Out More 29
    Books 29
    On the Internet 29
    Works Consulted 29
Glossary 31
Index 32

Words in bold type can be found in the glossary.

Hailee Steinfeld had just turned 14 in December 2010 when she attended the premiere of True Grit *in New York City.*

A Difficult Role

Joel and Ethan Coen had a big problem. The two brothers were directing a movie called *True Grit*. They needed to **cast** a teenage girl for the part of Mattie Ross. Mattie is the film's central character. She appears in almost every scene. The directors told the *Hollywood Reporter* that Mattie was "sassy, fearless, and sure of herself." Finding a young girl skilled enough to play that part would not be easy.

The Coen brothers **auditioned** more than 15,000 girls in late 2009. They looked at videos. They traveled around the country to meet actresses. No one was right for the part. "Ninety percent of the kids just get **eliminated** for one very obvious reason,"

Joel Coen told the *Hollywood Reporter*. "They're not actors in any sort of natural way."

Finally, just a month and a half before the movie started filming, the Coens

Hailee poses with her True Grit *buddies at a film festival in Germany in 2011: director Ethan Coen, actor Josh Brolin, director Joel Coen, and actor Jeff Bridges.*

auditioned a few girls in Los Angeles. One was a 13-year-old actress named Hailee Steinfeld. Hailee was not well known. In fact, she had only had a few small **roles** in movies and on TV.

When Hailee went to her audition, she was nervous. "Just the thought of it was kind of **intimidating**," she told the *Hollywood Reporter*. "But the minute I met [actor Jeff Bridges, the lead male character], I realized that he was there to do a job–and I'm there for the same reason."

Hailee's cool attitude was just what the Coen brothers were looking for. She was perfect for the role of Mattie.

When *True Grit* came out in 2010, it became a big hit. Hailee Steinfeld became a big star. Everyone was talking about the tough, smart, young actress. In the years that followed, Hailee would go on to great success in both movies and music. She became a rising star with plenty of talent.

Hailee and her family were delighted to attend the Academy Awards in 2011. Hailee poses with her father Peter, her mother Cheri, and her older brother Griffin on the red carpet before the event.

CHAPTER TWO

A Young Actress

Hailee Steinfeld was born on December 11, 1996, in Tarzana, California. She grew up in Thousand Oaks, just outside Los Angeles. Hailee's mom, Cheri, is an interior designer. Her father, Peter, is a personal fitness trainer. Hailee also has an older brother named Griffin, a race car driver. Hailee told the *New York Post* that her family's motto is "Have fun and don't take anything too seriously."

When Hailee was eight years old, she saw her older cousin working as an actress and a **model**. "To see my cousin doing that was really inspiring and I wanted to do it," Hailee told the Internet Movie Database. "So I went to my mom and I asked her if I could do it."

Hailee's parents made her take acting lessons for a year before she could try out for parts. Later, they hired an **agent** to get jobs for Hailee. Soon she was acting in commercials for companies like the Kmart store. She also did some modeling for The Gap clothing store.

Hailee moved on to small roles on television shows and movies. In 2007, she appeared in a Nickelodeon TV movie called *Summer Camp*. A year later, Hailee stopped going to public school. Instead, she was homeschooled. While homeschooling made it easier for Hailee to work as an actress, she told the *New York Post* that she left school because she was bullied. "It had nothing to do with acting," she said. "I don't know–everybody goes through it."

In 2008, Hailee appeared in a short film called *Heather: A Fairytale*. Hailee played the lead role of Heather. A year later, she starred as Talia Alden in another short film called *She's a Fox*. *She's a Fox* won several awards at **film festivals** around the United States.

Hailee has amazed audiences with her strong-willed performances in films. She was called a natural actress with a cool attitude by director Joel Coen.

2010 was a big year for Hailee. She appeared in two more short films, *Without Wings* and *Grand Cru*. And her biggest role was just around the corner.

Hailee starred as Mattie Ross, a tough-as-nails girl bent on revenge in the movie True Grit. *Her role in the movie made her an international star.*

True Grit

In 2010, Hailee won the role of Mattie Ross in *True Grit*. Hailee jumped right into her role as the tough, fast-talking teen who is bent on **revenge** for her father's killing. Mattie hires former lawman Rooster Cogburn, played by Jeff Bridges. He wasn't sure an unknown actress could handle the part. "To tell you the truth, I was very concerned about who was going to play that part, because it's a very difficult role," Bridges told *USA Today*.

Bridges stopped worrying after he and Hailee filmed their first scene together. "I was so relieved and happy that she was the star of our film," he continued. "The thing that was most impressive about Hailee is

Hailee was thrilled to work with Jeff Bridges, one of Hollywood's most popular actors, in True Grit. *The two became good friends during the filming.*

that she was able to get her tongue around those words and make it feel natural."

True Grit received great reviews. Richard Corliss of *Time* magazine called Hailee's performance one of the Top 10 Movie Performances of the Year. He wrote that she "stares down bad guys, wins hearts. That's a true gift."

In January 2011, *True Grit* was **nominated** for 10 Academy Awards. Hailee was nominated for Best Supporting Actress. She was asleep when the nominations were announced early in the morning. She found out the exciting news when she heard her parents cheering in another room. "That's how I woke up," she told the *New York Post*. "The first thing that I did, I started crying."

Hailee attended the Academy Awards, but she did not win an Oscar. However, she was thrilled at the experience. "Honestly, it's crazy," she told the Internet Movie Database. "It's such an amazing honor. . . . I'm proud to be a member of such an amazing cast–that's the best award of all."

Hailee's role as Juliet in Romeo and Juliet *was very different from the part of Mattie in* True Grit. *Hailee and her costar, Douglas Booth, arrive at the film's premiere in Hollywood in 2013.*

CHAPTER
FOUR

New Horizons

Hailee took a short break after *True Grit*, but she was soon back at work on other movies. In 2011, she was cast as Juliet in the film *Romeo and Juliet*. It was released in 2013.

That same year, Hailee played the role of Violet in the movie *Begin Again*. She also starred as Petra in *Ender's Game*, a science fiction action film based on a popular book. Filming *Ender's Game* was a difficult physical challenge, but Hailee enjoyed the work.

Over the next few years, Hailee **narrated** three **documentaries**: *Annie's Room, Letters to Jackie: Remembering President Kennedy*, and *Unity*.

The science fiction movie Ender's Game *required Hailee to perform many difficult physical feats, but she enjoyed trying something new. She appeared in July 2013 at San Diego's famous Comic-Con to help promote the film.*

Hailee's next big onscreen role was as Emily in *Pitch Perfect 2*. The film came out in 2015 and was very popular. Hailee sang a song called "Flashlight" in the movie. She discovered that she loved singing. She played some of her songs for Republic Records. In May 2015, Republic announced that it had signed a contract with Hailee

Hailee's fans loved her acting and singing in Pitch Perfect 2. *She signs autographs for a group of eager fans at the movie's world premiere in 2015.*

and she was working on new music for them.

The following month, Hailee and Shawn Mendes recorded an acoustic version of Shawn's hit song, "Stitches." One month later, Hailee released her first single, "Love Myself." At the end of 2015, she released an EP called *Haiz*.

In 2016, Hailee returned to the big screen in the movie *Term Life*. She also played the leading role of Nadine in *The Edge of Seventeen*. *The Edge of Seventeen* received good reviews and Hailee was nominated for a Golden Globe Award. The *New York Times* called the film, "one of the best films about high school kids in the past 25 years." The review praised Hailee, saying, "She manages a tricky balancing act, making Nadine [both] sympathetic and dislikable."

Music was also a big part of Hailee's life in 2016. She released the single "Starving" in July. The song was popular around the world and reached number 12 on the U.S. *Billboard* Hot 100 chart.

After her critically praised role as Nadine in The Edge of Seventeen, *Hailee attends the Critics' Choice Awards in 2016.*

Hailee didn't slow down in 2017. She began filming *Pitch Perfect 3*. She also recorded several singles with Machine Gun Kelly and Prince Fox.

Hailee's success in music was rewarded with an award at the Billboard Women in Music event in 2016. She hosted and performed at the show as well.

CHAPTER FIVE

Hailee's Real Life

Hailee continues to try new things. In December 2016, she hosted and performed at the *Billboard* Women in Music Awards. The event featured performances by many of music's most popular female stars, including Halsey, Alessia Cara, Maren Morris, and Andra Day.

Early in 2017, Hailee was named the new face of the Reef Escape sandal collection. Hailee was eager to represent the brand. She told *Vogue*, "There have always been a bunch of sandals at the bottom of the stairs right by the front door that were my go-to. They were always Reef. I grew up wearing these sandals." Hailee also explained that she was becoming more aware of fashion as she grew older.

Hailee Steinfeld may be famous, but at heart she is just a normal young woman. She told the Internet Movie Database, "Child actors come off as work being their life and doing it 24/7, but I still have those days where it's totally, like, whatever: shopping, movies, adventures." She has close friends outside of the music and movie industries and enjoys spending time with her family as well.

Giving back and helping others is also an important part of Hailee's life. She has joined the No Kid Hungry campaign to end child hunger in the United States. She also supports an anti-bullying charity called the Trevor Project.

In the future, Hailee hopes to direct movies as well as star in them. She also plans to continue her music career. "I realize how fortunate I am to have found what I love so young," she told the Internet Movie Database.

Charity work is important to Hailee. She waves to fans at a Hollywood event for the charity Stand Up 2 Cancer.

Hailee loves to perform her music. Here she has fun performing at CBS Radio's SPF concert in Las Vegas in May 2017.

Hailee tries to take her life one day at a time. "I don't have a specific place I want to be or know where I'm going to be five years from now," she said. Wherever that place is, it's a sure thing that Hailee will be a star.

CHRONOLOGY

1996 Hailee Steinfeld is born in Tarzana, California, on December 11.

2007 Appears in the Nickelodeon TV movie *Summer Camp.*

2008 Appears in her first short film, *Heather: A Fairytale.*

2009 Appears in the short film *She's a Fox.*

2010 Appears as Mattie Ross in *True Grit.*

2011 Nominated for Best Supporting Actress for *True Grit.*

2013 Makes several movies, including *Romeo and Juliet* and *Ender's Game.*

2015 Appears as Emily in *Pitch Perfect 2*; releases the song "Love Myself"; releases music EP *Haiz.*

2016 Appears in *The Edge of Seventeen*; releases the song "Starving."

2017 Begins filming *Pitch Perfect 3.*

FILMOGRAPHY

2008 *Heather: A Fairytale*

2009 *She's a Fox*

2010 *Without Wings*
Grand Cru
True Grit

2013 *The Magic Bracelet*
Hateship, Loveship
Begin Again
Romeo and Juliet
Ender's Game

2014 *Three Days to Kill*
The Homesman
The Keeping Room

2015 *Ten Thousand Saints*
Pitch Perfect 2
Barely Lethal

2016 *Term Life*
The Edge of Seventeen

2017 *Pitch Perfect 3*

FIND OUT MORE

Books

Beck, Lowell. *Hailee Steinfeld: The Biography*. Kindle edition. Seattle, WA: Amazon Digital Services, 2016.

Portis, Charles. *True Grit: Young Readers Edition*. New York: Overlook Press, 2016.

On the Internet

Hailee Steinfeld Bio. Kidzworld.com http://www.kidzworld.com/article/25385-hailee-steinfeld-bio

Hailee Steinfeld Biography. Aceshowbiz.com http://www.aceshowbiz.com/celebrity/hailee_steinfled/biography.html

Hailee Steinfeld Biography. Internet Movie Database http://www.imdb.com/name/nm2794962/bio

Works Consulted

Corliss, Richard. "The Top 10 Everything of 2010–Hailee Steinfeld as Mattie Ross in True Grit." *Time*, December 9, 2010. http://content.time.com/time/specials/packages/article/0,28804,2035319_2035307_2032773,00.html

"Hailee Steinfeld to Host and Perform at *Billboard* Women in Music 2016." *Billboard*, December 5, 2016. http://www.billboard.com/articles/events/women-in-music/7597424/hailee-steinfeld-host-billboard-women-in-music

FIND OUT MORE

Holden, Stephen. "Review: The Edge of Seventeen Takes Teenage Movies to a Higher Place." *New York Times*, November 17, 2016. https://www.nytimes.com/2016/11/18/movies/the-edge-of-seventeen-review-hailee-steinfeld.html?_r=0

Longwell, Todd. "The Story Behind the Casting of 'True Grit's' Hailee Steinfeld." *Hollywood Reporter*, January 7, 2011. http://www.hollywoodreporter.com/news/story-casting-true-grits-hailee-69535

Mandell, Andrea. "Hailee's Next Frontier: Oscar. But First, the Mall." *USA Today*, February 2, 2011. http://usatoday30.usatoday.com/life/movies/movieawards/oscars/2011-02-02-Steinfeld02_CV_N.htm

Okwodu, Janelle. "Hailee Steinfeld on Flip Flops and Dressing for the Red Carpet." *Vogue*, January 30, 2017. http://www.vogue.com/article/hailee-steinfeld-reefs-collection-interview

Stadtmiller, Mandy. "'Grit' Girl." *New York Post*, February 20, 2011. http://nypost.com/2011/02/20/grit-girl/

PHOTO CREDITS: Cover, pp. 1, 3–Ilya S. Savenok/Stringer/Getty Images for A+E/Getty Images Entertainment; p. 4–Jemal Countess/Staff/Getty Images Entertainment; p. 6–Andreas Rentz/Staff/Getty Images for Paramount Pictures/Getty Images Entertainment; p. 8–© Paul Fenton/ZUMAPRESS.com/ZUMA Press, Inc./Alamy Stock Photo; p. 10–Robert Delgadillo/cc by-sa 3.0 Unported/OTRS; pp. 12, 14–Collection Christophel/Alamy Stock Photo; p. 16–Jason Merritt/Staff/Getty Images Entertainment; p. 18–Joe Scarnici/Stringer/Getty Images for Summit Entertainment/Getty Images Entertainment; p. 19–Alex J. Berliner/(ABImages) via AP Images/ASSOCIATED PRESS; p. 21–Mike Windle/Staff/Getty Images for The Critics' Choice Awards/Getty Images Entertainment; p. 22–Nicholas Hunt/Staff/Getty Images for Billboard Magazine/Getty Images Entertainment; p. 25–Frederick M. Brown/Stringer/Getty Images Entertainment; p. 26–Isaac Brekken/Stringer/Getty Images for CBS Radio Inc./Getty Images Entertainment.

GLOSSARY

agent (AY-jent)–a person who finds work for other people

auditioned (aw-DISH-und)–tried out for a part in a show or movie

cast (KAST)–to choose actors and actresses for parts in a show or movie

documentaries (dok-yoo-MEN-tuh-reez)–movies or TV shows that are factual reports

eliminated (ee-LIM-uh-nay-ted)–got rid of

film festivals (FILM FES-tuh-vuhlz)–organized series of movies held in the same place

intimidating (in-TIM-uh-day-ting)–frightening

model (MAH-duhl)–a person who wears clothes to display them for a designer or a company

narrated (NAIR-ay-ted)–told in speech

nominated (NOM-uh-nay-ted)–selected to try out for an award

revenge (ree-VENJ)–to hurt someone for an injury or wrong they have done

roles (ROLLZ)– parts in shows or movies

INDEX

Academy Awards 15
Annie's Room 17
Begin Again 17
Billboard Women in Music Awards 23
Bridges, Jeff 7, 13, 14
Coen, Ethan 5
Coen, Joel 5, 6
Edge of Seventeen, The 20
Ender's Game 17
Grand Cruz 11
Haiz 20
Heather: A Fairytale 10
Letters to Jackie 17
Mendes, Shawn 20
Pitch Perfect 2 18
Pitch Perfect 3 21
Reef Escape 23
Republic Records 18
Romeo and Juliet 17
Ross, Mattie 5, 7, 13
She's a Fox 10
Steinfeld, Cheri 9
Steinfeld, Griffin 9
Steinfeld, Hailee
- birth of 9
- early acting career of 10–11
- homeschooling of 10
- auditions for *True Grit* 7
- appears in *True Grit* 13–15
- nominated for an Academy Award 15
- appears in movies 17, 20
- narrates documentaries 17
- appears in *Pitch Perfect 2* 18
- begins singing career 18
- releases music 20
- appears in *The Edge of Seventeen* 20
- films *Pitch Perfect 3* 21
- represents Reef Escape sandal collection 23
- charity work and 24

Steinfeld, Peter 9
Summer Camp 10
Term Life 20
True Grit 5–7, 13, 15, 17
Unity 17
Without Wings 11